MCPL - 15616 E. 24 HWY.
INDEPENDENCE, MO 64050

3001000298720 7

Alpine, Rachele   JE ALPINE
Art with heart

10538833

WITHDRAWN
FROM THE RECORDS OF THE
MID-CONTINENT PUBLIC LIBRARY

 Art with Heart

Don't miss the other
Invincible Girls Club adventures!

Home Sweet Forever Home

THE INVINCIBLE GIRLS ♥ CLUB

♥ BOOK 2 ♥

ART WITH HEART

by Rachele Alpine

illustrated by Addy Rivera Sonda

Aladdin

New York   London   Toronto   Sydney   New Delhi

This book is a work of fiction. Any references to historical events, real people, or real places are used fictitiously. Other names, characters, places, and events are products of the author's imagination, and any resemblance to actual events or places or persons, living or dead, is entirely coincidental.

ALADDIN
An imprint of Simon & Schuster Children's Publishing Division
1230 Avenue of the Americas, New York, New York 10020
First Aladdin hardcover edition May 2021
Text copyright © 2021 by Rachele Alpine
Illustrations copyright © 2021 by Addy Rivera Sonda
Also available in an Aladdin paperback edition.
All rights reserved, including the right of reproduction in whole or in part in any form.
ALADDIN and related logo are registered trademarks of Simon & Schuster, Inc.
For information about special discounts for bulk purchases, please contact
Simon & Schuster Special Sales at 1-866-506-1949 or business@simonandschuster.com.
The Simon & Schuster Speakers Bureau can bring authors to your live event. For
more information or to book an event contact the Simon & Schuster Speakers Bureau
at 1-866-248-3049 or visit our website at www.simonspeakers.com.
Book designed by Heather Palisi
The illustrations for this book were rendered digitally.
The text of this book was set in Celeste.
Manufactured in the United States of America 0321 FFG
2 4 6 8 10 9 7 5 3 1
Library of Congress Cataloging-in-Publication Data
Names: Alpine, Rachele, 1979- author. | Sonda, Addy Rivera, illustrator.
Title: Art with heart / by Rachele Alpine ; illustrated by Addy Rivera Sonda.
Description: First Aladdin paperback edition. | New York : Aladdin, 2021. |
Series: The Invincible Girls Club ; book 2 | Audience: Ages 7 to 10. |
Summary: Emelyn and her three best friends use positive words and art to fight back against bullying at school.
Identifiers: LCCN 2021000528 (print) | LCCN 2021000529 (ebook) |
ISBN 9781534475335 (hc) | ISBN 9781534475328 (pbk) | ISBN 9781534475342 (ebook)
Subjects: CYAC: Bullying—Fiction. | Kindness—Fiction. |
Friendship—Fiction. | Schools—Fiction.
Classification: LCC PZ7.A46255 Ar 2021 (print) | LCC PZ7.A46255 (ebook) |
DDC [Fic]—dc23
LC record available at https://lccn.loc.gov/2021000528
LC ebook record available at https://lccn.loc.gov/2021000529

For my grandma Dorothy Hoeffler,
whose art fills me with memories and love

*Art is something that makes you breathe
with a different kind of happiness.*
-Anni Albers

Contents

ORANGE YOU GLAD YOU'RE NOT IN TROUBLE

"Emelyn," my teacher Miss Taylor said. "I need you to go to the office."

I froze, the tip of my pencil dangling over the math problem I'd been working on.

The office?

Okay, maybe I hadn't exactly been *working* on the math problems. I might have been doodling a picture of a cat, but that couldn't get me sent to the principal's office, right?

My classmates stopped what they were doing and turned toward me.

There was nothing worse than having the attention focused on you.

And right then everyone stared at me as if I were the most popular animal at the zoo.

I played with the cuff of my jean jacket and stared at the glittery nail polish I had put on the night before. What I didn't look at was my class-mates.

"Ohhhhhhhhhhh, Emelyn is in trouble," Nelson said in the most obnoxious voice in the world.

"Mind your own business!" my best friend Myka said. "She's not in trouble."

Myka was the most outspoken of the Invincible Girls, which was a club my three friends and I had started in order to make the world a better place. Right then I was grateful for Myka's support. With three brothers, she was a pro at standing up for her-self. Myka didn't let anyone push her or her friends around.

I mouthed *Thank you* to her for silencing Nelson, because she was right. I wasn't in trouble.

At least, I didn't think I was.

Wouldn't you know if you were in trouble?

My brain switched into overdrive as I tried to come up with a reason, any reason, as to why I would be sent to the principal's office.

Sure, I was drawing during math, but I paid attention. I swear I did. Drawing helped me focus, and Miss Taylor had always been cool with that.

"Nelson, that's enough," Miss Taylor said, and she turned to me and held up an envelope. "I was hoping you'd run something to the office. It needs to get there now, and you're one of the most responsible students in the class."

She said that last part as she looked right at Nelson, who was nowhere close to the most responsible.

"So I'm not in trouble?" I asked.

Miss Taylor laughed. "Not at all. Quite the opposite."

It was as if the gray storm clouds whooshed away and the clear blue sky filled with rainbows, unicorns, and birds who chirped happy songs.

I was not in trouble!

I repeat, I was not in trouble!

"Thank you," Miss Taylor said as I took the envelope she held out to me. "I figured I could trust you."

"You sure can," I said, and heard someone

snicker. I didn't stick around to find out if it was Nelson and his big mouth. I zipped out the door as Miss Taylor told the class once more to focus on their work.

The hallway was empty, which was weird.

The classroom doors were closed, and while I could hear the sound of voices, I couldn't make out any of the words.

Squeak, squeak, squeak.

The bottoms of my shoes rubbed against the shiny floor.

I glanced down at them and grinned.

It was silly to get excited about a pair of shoes, but I loved mine so much. Mom had let me paint a white pair of sneakers we had found at the discount store. I made one hot pink and the other purple. I had added sequins and glitter and neon-green laces. They were the coolest shoes ever, especially since no one else in the entire universe had them. I was all about wearing one-of-a-kind creations. Myka called my style the nacho style.

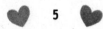

"It's like the nachos my mom makes. She loads a little bit of this and a little bit of that and then a ton of cheese, and somehow they're perfect!" Myka had said to explain the name.

She was right. Today, along with my shoes, I had on cute, flowy, white wide-legged pants, a tank top with polka dots, and Mom's old jean jacket. My socks didn't match, but then again, I hardly ever bothered to match my socks. Who had time for that?

I did a twirl down the hall and imagined myself about to make my grand entrance at a ball.

A royal ball.

Yep, I was a princess headed to the fanciest party of the year.

This was my kingdom, and behind each door, people prepared to celebrate.

I closed my eyes and imagined the scene I would draw. A giant room full of windows and mirrors. Bright pieces of silk fabric would stretch across the ceiling, banners would hang from the walls, and candles would flicker on tables.

Mom said I had the best imagination of anyone she knew, and that was why my art was so incredible. I don't know about the incredible part, but I do love to draw. There is nothing more fun than picturing something in my head and then bringing it to life on paper.

Right then that picture was a far-off kingdom. I was so lost in this world that I didn't notice the wet spot on the floor in the world right in front of me.

Whoosh!

My foot slipped and I went flying.

I threw my arms up to catch my balance, which worked. But the envelope dropped and slid under the door to the janitor's closet.

"Great," I said to myself. "Now you really *are* going to get yourself in trouble."

I was reaching out to see if the door was unlocked, when the envelope shot back out from the little space between the bottom of the door and the floor.

Um, what?

I rubbed at my eyes.

Had I really seen that?

What in the world had just happened?

My mind flashed back to the castle scene I had imagined. Maybe there was a dragon hiding behind the door. I couldn't decide if that was cool or terrifying.

Or more likely there was a vent in the closet or some other boring explanation like that.

I inspected the envelope for dragon slime, but nothing looked out of the ordinary.

"Get your head back into reality, Emelyn," I said. I needed to deliver this envelope, so there was no time to hang around and figure out who or what was in the closet.

Suddenly there was a noise.

A sniffle-hiccup kind of noise.

A noise like someone crying.

And it came from the closet.

What should I do?

Miss Taylor had picked me to deliver this envelope, and there was no way I was going to let her down.

But someone was upset. I couldn't walk away, could I? What if something was wrong and the person needed help?

"You know what to do," I whispered. "You're an Invincible Girl."

I knocked on the door.

Maybe it was silly to knock, but if there was a dragon or some other creature in there, I wasn't about to upset them.

"Hello. I'm not here to cause trouble. I wanted to thank you for giving me back my envelope," I said, but there was no response. "I hope you don't mind, but I'm going to open the door to make sure you're okay."

When I still didn't get a reply, I put my hand on the knob and turned.

"Be brave, be brave, be brave," I chanted as I mustered up the courage to find out who or . . . gulp . . . what was hiding in the closet.

The door swung open, and there, in the shadowy dark, two eyes blinked back at me!

SEEING RED

M y body tensed, and I waited for the creature to come out of the closet and gobble me up. The ferocious dragon looking for a meal!

But that didn't happen.

I'd had it wrong.

It wasn't a monster or a dragon.

Instead of belonging to a monster with sharp teeth and scaly skin, the eyes belonged to a girl in the same grade as me. She was in a different class, but I knew her name was Chelsea. And she wasn't breathing fire or roaring at me. She sat on the ground, her arms wrapped around her knees and her cheeks wet from tears.

"Chelsea? What's wrong?" I asked. "Are you okay?"

She didn't answer.

"What is that?" I pointed to the wadded pieces of paper on the ground that surrounded her.

"Nothing," she said. She took off her glasses and swiped the back of her hand across her eyes.

But it was obviously something. Why else would she be so upset?

I picked up two of the pieces of paper and smoothed them out. I hoped I wasn't being nosy, but I wanted to help. No one liked to see someone cry.

As soon as I read the pages, I understood why she was so upset.

The words on the papers were mean. One note was about how Chelsea was stuck-up, and the other said her laugh sounded like a donkey. Mom always reminded me that if I didn't have anything nice to say, then I shouldn't say anything at all. And the person who had written these messages should have kept their mouth shut.

"Where did you find these?" I asked.

"They're everywhere," Chelsea said as she sniffled. "Someone stuck them on the lockers, the walls, and even in the bathroom. I didn't know what to do. I needed to get away from them, and this seemed like the only place where there weren't any."

I peeked into the hallway, and sure enough, there were squares of bright-colored paper. Not a ton, but enough to catch someone's attention if they weren't lost in a daydream about princes and princesses and protecting one's village from mythical creatures—or other classmates.

"There's stuff written about a lot of people. I'm not the only one," she said.

"We need to tell someone. This is bullying." I thought about our school's policy. No one was allowed to bully, and you could get in serious trouble for it.

"I don't know who did it," Chelsea said.

"Maybe not, but we can stop what they were trying to do before anyone else discovers it," I declared.

I took the notes and ripped them into tiny shreds. Whoever had written these messages was worse than any dragon I could've found behind the closet door.

"Do you want to pull them down with me?" I

14

still had the envelope to deliver, but first I had to get rid of these messages.

Chelsea nodded. "I don't want anyone else to see them."

"Me either. Let's throw them into the trash, where they belong."

I reached my hand out to help her up. Chelsea grabbed it and stood. Together we raced through the school and pulled down the papers. At first we wadded them up and threw them away. But soon we were ripping them into tiny pieces before tossing them into the trash. And wow, did that feel good.

We searched each and every one out and destroyed them.

"Woo-hoo!" I cheered as I dropped the pieces like confetti. "Another one bites the dust!"

"See you later, alligator!" Chelsea exclaimed, and yanked one off the wall.

"After a while, crocodile," I said, and did the same.

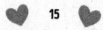

15

We made it a game, growing sillier and sillier about it. As we did, a strange thing happened. Instead of being upset, the two of us were laughing. And kind of having fun.

As we destroyed the messages, I realized I'd had it wrong. I'd never been the princess. I was the brave knight. And together with fellow knight Chelsea, I was using my sword to slice through each and every one of those messages. We had slain the dragon and banished it from the kingdom.

"It felt so good to take those down," Chelsea said.

"And even better to rip them up," I added.

"You've got that right!"

The two of us looped past the office on the way back to our classrooms. I dropped off the envelope, and then the two of us filled the school secretary, Ms. Blume, in about the notes around the school.

"Goodness," she said, and let out a giant sigh. "This wasn't what I wanted to hear. You're not the first to report notes like this. I had hoped it was over. I'll let Ms. Álvarez know."

That made me feel a tiny bit better. Ms. Álvarez was our principal, and she would make sure that the notes stopped. She hated bullying.

She wrote us each a pass, and we headed back to class. I was glad Chelsea and I had made certain that no one else would see the words that had hung all over the school, but I hated that these weren't the first of them. I hoped the ones we'd pulled down were the last.

"Thank you for everything," Chelsea said when we got to her classroom.

"Are you kidding? I'm happy to help keep the kingdom safe," I said.

"The kingdom?" she asked, and raised an eyebrow.

"I mean the school. I'm glad we put a stop to whoever wrote those messages."

We said goodbye, and I slipped into my classroom as quietly as possible. Miss Taylor caught my eye and mouthed, *Everything okay?* I had been gone a long time, a lot longer than I should have been to just take a note to the office. I nodded and sat back at my desk and stared at the math problems I had been working on before I'd left. But I couldn't concentrate, because in my pocket was a crumpled sheet of paper with a mean message directed at me.

I don't know why I hadn't ripped it up and tossed it into the garbage like the other messages, but even if I had, it probably wouldn't have helped. The words would still be stuck in my head. Words that reminded me that sometimes when you thought you had banished the dragon, it came thundering back and burned you with its fire.

3 THE CURATOR OF GOOD ADVICE

"Attention, hello, is anyone there?" Mom asked as she waved her hand in front of my face at the kitchen table that night. We had both changed into our pajamas after dinner and had bowls of ice cream in front of us. "Is everything okay?"

"Uh-huh," I said as I stirred the ice cream around in my bowl. It had melted into a sticky, soupy mess. But what I'd said wasn't true. Things weren't okay. I could not stop thinking about those messages. The one about me, the ones about my classmates, and any future ones that might pop up.

"Are you sure?" she asked. "Because you haven't touched your dessert. I've never seen that happen."

"Just a lot on my mind," I replied as I pushed away my bowl. "I think I'll head to bed."

"Okay, now I'm positive that something is wrong," Mom responded. "You never pass up ice cream, and it's only six thirty. We haven't even watched our game shows yet. Do you want me to make some waves?"

"Making waves" was our signal to talk. Mom would wet my hair and then separate it into tiny braids. I'd sleep on them, and in the morning when we took them out, my hair would look like I'd spent the day at the beach and my worries had gotten "swept away by the ocean," as Mom said.

"You might need to," I told her. While I didn't feel like talking, her company would probably be a good thing.

 21

"How many braids am I going to need to make tonight?" Mom asked.

"A million," I told her, which was code for saying that what was bothering me was a big deal.

"Lucky for you, I've been wanting to make a million braids."

"Yeah, right."

"Totally," she joked.

I cracked a smile. I loved Mom. She always knew how to make it better.

"Okay," I said. "But I'm telling you, this isn't going to be an easy job."

"It never is," she said, and pulled out the beanbag chairs we kept in our family room. "Grab a seat. I'll be right back."

I settled into a lime-green beanbag and waited for Mom. When we'd moved in, the first thing we'd done was paint the walls. And not boring colors like the beiges and yellows the apartment had already had. No, we wanted color. Bright colors. That was how our living room had become lavender, our kitchen turquoise, and Mom's bathroom magenta.

"To match the streaks in your hair," Mom had said as we'd painted, which was true. Mom was a hairstylist and had colored my hair a deep purple a few days before our move.

Our apartment was a color explosion, which usually put me in a better mood, but tonight even that wasn't helping.

Mom returned with a spray bottle, brush, and giant bag of mini rubber bands. She held them up.

"I told you I was ready to make a million braids."

"You might not need to make that many," I said, inspecting the bag. "We'll be here all week if you use every one of those."

"Let's just get started and see how it goes."

She pulled out my ponytail and began to brush. I closed my eyes and relaxed. There's just something about someone doing your hair that feels so good.

 23

But try as I might, I couldn't shake the twisty, curvy feeling that I got every time I thought about the messages.

I let out a shaky sigh. One that was a few seconds away from me bursting out in tears.

"Still thinking about things?" Mom asked.

"Yep," I said.

"Anything I can help with?"

"I don't think so," I told her. "It's school stuff."

"Perfect! I went to school back in the day, so I know a thing or two."

"You also have an oven, but you're no gourmet chef," I pointed out.

"Hey! I take offense at that. I provide you with incredible meals," Mom said.

"Yeah, from take-out places."

"Okay, now we're getting technical."

The two of us laughed. A real genuine laugh that didn't feel forced.

"It's just that someone wrote some really awful messages about me and my classmates and stuck them up around the school," I said.

"A message about you?" Mom asked.

I nodded. "Yeah, and my friends, too."

"Does your teacher know?" Mom asked, and I nodded.

"Yep, and my friends and I took the messages

down and told Ms. Blume. I guess this isn't the first time someone's done this."

Mom let go of the section of hair she was braiding and gave me a giant hug. "I'm so proud of you for taking them down and then telling someone. That takes courage."

"Thanks," I said. "I just feel awful, because the words were really mean."

"Words can be powerful," Mom said. "But you can change that power around."

"How?" I asked.

"Spread positive words instead. Remind people of the good things about them," she suggested. "For example, when I look at you, I see a girl who is creative and kind. Someone who cares about others. I could fill an entire notebook full of positive things. *Those* are the words you want to focus on and carry around in your head and heart."

Mom touched the tip of her finger to my head and the spot on my chest where my heart was to emphasize her point.

"Remind your classmates of that," she said.

"You're always so smart," I told her.

"I know," she agreed, and the two of us burst out laughing.

How was it that Mom could always make me feel better, even when I felt at my worst?

4 A PICTURE IS WORTH A THOUSAND WORDS

Each member of the Invincible Girls Club had her own way of dealing with hard stuff.

Myka kicked the soccer ball against her garage, Lauren watched videos of baby animals on the internet, and Ruby wrote in her journal.

My solution was drawing. I could get lost in the world I created and not think about anything else for hours. One of the most magical parts was that when I was done, I almost always felt better. Whatever was making me upset might not have disappeared, but I was able to handle it. Art calmed me.

So that's exactly what I did after Mom finished braiding my hair. I gave her a kiss, thanked her for talking with me, and headed to my room.

I suddenly had a plan, and I needed to immediately put it into action.

I stepped into my room and instantly relaxed. I might have been the only kid in the world who wanted to get sent to her room.

We lived in an apartment building, and Mom had let me have the room that opened to a balcony, where I kept the telescope my grandparents had given me for my birthday. I was kind of obsessed with space, so now I could check out what was going on in the universe whenever I wanted!

I had chosen a blue ombré color for my bedroom walls, which meant it started from dark blue on the ceiling and went all the way to a light blue color. I'd had a whole vision going when I'd designed the wall, so we'd taken sponges, dipped them in white paint, and added clouds. Mom had helped string white lights around the balcony and stick about a million glow-in-the-dark stars on the ceiling. When I lay in my bed, it was as if I were floating in space!

The rest of my room was filled with a giant table.

I didn't even have a dresser because the table was so gigantic.

It wasn't a big deal, though, because the table was the perfect workstation for an artist.

We'd found it at one of the flea markets Mom liked to go to on the weekends when she didn't have to work. She called going to flea markets "treasure hunting," although I'd never found anything I would consider a treasure. That is, until I'd spotted my table.

It had taken a bit of begging, but finally Mom had agreed to let me take it home.

I kept my supplies on it in old bottles and

containers that Mom and I recycled. There were trays for paper, and a bookshelf where I saved my sketchbooks. The neatest part was that the table was a work of art itself. It was covered in pen marks, paint, gouges from scissors, glue, and other bits and pieces left behind from projects I had worked on.

I powered on my tablet and picked my favorite playlist in the world. I called it my Invincible Girls Mix. It was full of songs that celebrated girl power and how awesome girls are. I cranked it up super loud, because I needed those positive lyrics right then.

I took the crumpled slip of paper out of my book bag and smoothed it on the table.

Now, after I read the words over again, I wished I hadn't.

Emelyn's hair looks like a rainbow threw up on her head.

The message was silly, but still, the words hurt as much as they had the first time I'd read them.

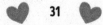 31

I loved the colors Mom put in my hair. I'd always thought my hair was fun and special. So why would someone write something so mean?

I wadded up the slip of paper with the awful words about me on it. I tossed it into the garbage, which was what I should have done when I'd first found it.

I thought about what Mom had said when she'd been braiding my hair. She'd told me I was kind, caring, and creative—words that were a million times better than what the note said about my hair.

I took out a fresh sheet of paper, and in the middle I wrote, *Emelyn is . . .*

Then, just like the playlist I was listening to, I decided to create my own Invincible Girls Mix. First I wrote the words Mom had used to describe me. After that I added words of my own:

A good friend.

An artist.

Obsessed with outer space.

A volunteer.

A lover of color.

Imaginative.

Smart.

A future astronaut.

A dreamer.

A storyteller.

A daughter.

A girl with nacho style.

I filled the page with positive words about myself.

Words that made me proud.

Words I'd *want* to see on a note written about me.

"That's it!" I said out loud. I had had a flash of brilliance.

I grabbed another sheet of paper, and in the center I wrote, *Chelsea is . . .* and decorated it with stars and swirls. I wrote tons of words to describe how I saw her. Words to cancel out the mean stuff on the messages she had found.

Then I made three more pages. One each for Myka, Lauren, and Ruby.

I hung mine on the bulletin board above my art table and smiled.

These were the words that described me.

Strong words.

Powerful words.

Words that made me feel invincible.

CHALK THIS UP
TO A GREAT IDEA

5

There were so many ways people could react to art. Luckily for me, Chelsea loved the drawing I'd made her.

"This is the nicest thing ever!" she said, and clutched it to her chest.

I tried not to grin too big, but it was hard. Doing nice things for others is the best way to make yourself happy.

"I made one for me, too," I told her. "I hung it on the wall in my room. That way I can look at it

35

and remember the good things instead of those awful messages we took down."

"That's a great idea! I'm going to tape this to the inside cover of my notebook, so I can peek at it during the school day." She held the drawing out in front of her to look at it again.

"I'm glad you like it," I said.

"You totally made my day," she said.

And that was why art was the most incredible thing in the world. It could change the way a person felt or viewed something. It was like performing a magic trick on paper.

I couldn't wait to give my friends their drawings.

I held on to them until the next day, which was Saturday. We always spent that day together in the best possible way.

First we volunteered at the dog shelter in their Paws for Reading program. We helped out with anything that needed to be done and read to the dogs. Then we went to Sprinkle & Shine.

It was a cupcake shop owned by Lauren's uncle Patrick, which meant endless treats to feast on!

This Saturday was no exception. We had a great time at the kennel and then settled in at Sprinkle & Shine for some major cupcake consumption.

"Well, well, well, hello, delicious. We meet again!" Myka said as she unwrapped the cupcake in front of her. "Fancy seeing you here. Now get into my belly!"

She ate the mini cupcake in three bites and reached for another. I grabbed another one too, because who could resist a plate full of cupcakes?

"The new dogs in the shelter this week were adorable," Ruby said.

"The dogs are always adorable there," Lauren corrected her. "I wish I could take every one of them home!"

"Your stepdad would blow the roof off your house with his sneezes," Myka said, which was true. Lauren's stepdad was very allergic to dogs, which stunk for her, because she was the biggest dog lover in the world.

I pulled out my drawings as my friends continued to joke with each other.

"I have a surprise for all of you," I said shyly. I was excited to give them the pictures, but also nervous. What if they thought it was silly?

But then again, what if they loved their pictures like Chelsea had?

That gave me courage to reach into my bag and hand out the rolls of paper I had tied with ribbons.

"Ohhhhh . . . I love surprises!" Myka said.

"It's nothing big," I said. "Just something I made the other day."

I nervously waited as they opened their drawings and began to read.

"Emelyn! This is too something big!" Ruby said, and waved her sheet in the air. She read out loud some of the things I'd written. "Ruby is a great friend, caring, a leader, inquisitive, outspoken, a good writer, and an amazing cook."

"What about mine?" Lauren said. "I'm a dog lover, animal protector, brave, loyal, best friend, honest. I love a good challenge and am confident, dependable, and always ready to help."

"Well, I'm athletic, determined, a great sister, silly, a math superstar, strong, tough, and optimistic," Myka said. "You forgot to add 'future gold-medal winner,' but it's okay, I'll forgive you."

"Whoops! How could I forget that?" I joked, and held out the markers I'd brought, and my own drawing with my name. "Actually, I was thinking maybe we could swap drawings and write a few more words about each other. You know, like a collage of kindness."

"A collage of kindness! I love that idea," Ruby said, and picked the purple marker and reached over for Myka's paper. "Here, Myka. I'll add 'gold-medal winner.'"

"How did you think of this?" Lauren asked.

"I made one for Chelsea and myself after finding mean messages that someone put up." I filled the girls in on what had happened two days ago. "They were awful. My mom suggested that it might help to look at positive words. You know, to cancel out the negative stuff."

"I heard someone talking about the mean notes the other day," Lauren said.

"I guess this isn't the first time it's happened," I told them.

"Wait, there was stuff written about you?" Myka asked.

"There was stuff written about a lot of people in our grade," I said, and wrinkled my nose in disgust.

"What!" Myka shouted so loud that a few people turned around and stared. "Why didn't you say something at school?"

"I don't know. I guess I didn't want to think about it," I said.

"Well, we're not going to forget," Myka said. "No one messes with my best friend!"

Ruby took her fist and banged it on the table. I jumped, surprised by the noise.

"All right," she said. "I call this meeting of the Invincible Girls Club to order. It's been two weeks since we found eight adorable, sweet, cuddly, lovable dogs homes. Two weeks since we used our powers for good and worked to change the world. Which is two weeks too long, in my opinion."

"What are you doing?" Lauren asked. "We were in the middle of an important conversation."

"Exactly, and I have our next mission," Ruby

said. "As Invincible Girls, it's our duty to stand up against whoever wrote those messages."

Myka bounced around, full of excitement. "Of course! You're right! Invincible Girls would never ignore this."

"But what can we do? No one knows who wrote those messages," I said.

"Didn't we ask 'But what can we do' about the dogs?" Myka asked. "Haven't we learned not to doubt ourselves?"

"We need to think outside the box," Lauren said, and we groaned. It was one of Miss Taylor's favorite phrases. She said it inspired "creative thinking" and "brilliant ideas."

"We need to kill them with kindness," I added, and my friends groaned even louder. That was another one of Miss Taylor's favorite phrases.

"Seriously, though," Lauren said. "We need to come up with something the teachers haven't thought of yet. We did it with the dogs; we can do it here, too."

Before we could say anything else, Lauren's uncle came to our table with another plate full of cupcakes.

"Do you have room to taste-test the new flavor I created?" he said. He had a red-and-white-striped apron on over his jeans, and a mint-green bow tie. "I think I've got it, but it seems to be missing something—that last perfect burst of flavor. Anyone interested in figuring out what that could be?"

"Nah, I'm not into cupcakes," Myka said. "I was hoping for a giant plate of steamed veggies."

"Oh, my apologies. I can make that happen," Uncle Patrick said, and he turned and headed toward the kitchen.

"Stop! Wait! I was kidding!" Myka said. "Come back with the sweets! Please!"

He pivoted around on his foot and in two steps reached the table and put the platter down. "Introducing blueberry pancake cupcakes."

"Pancake?" Ruby asked. "That sounds delicious!"

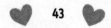

"You do know I'm the pancake-eating champ in my house, right?" Myka said. "I can eat them faster than anyone else, which comes in handy when you have brothers who practically inhale the entire stack."

"Wait until you get to the middle," Uncle Patrick said, and bounced on his toes. I loved the way he got excited about his cupcakes. It reminded me of how I got when I created a new picture.

"Is that maple syrup?" Lauren asked after a few bites.

"You betcha it is!" Uncle Patrick said, and clapped with delight.

"Get out!" Myka yelled, and popped her cupcake into her mouth. "This is my new all-time favorite!"

Ruby paused and tapped her finger against her temple as if thinking. "These are excellent, but you're right. They're missing something important."

"That special touch, right?" Uncle Patrick said. "That thing that takes the cupcake from amazing and elevates it to the best cupcake ever made in the universe!"

"Lucky for you, I know what it is," Ruby said.

"Do tell!" Uncle Patrick said, and he leaned close to Ruby, as if she were about to let him in on top secret information.

"Bacon," Ruby said with a smug look on her face.

"Mmmm, bacon," Myka said.

"Yep!" Ruby said. "I'm a firm believer that putting bacon on anything makes it incredible. And this cupcake is missing that key ingredient."

Uncle Patrick scratched his chin and nodded. "Ruby, you're a genius. That's exactly what it needs!"

Ruby beamed. "I'm happy to test out the first batch! And the second and third!"

"I'll make a bunch with your name on them," he said.

"And maybe a few without bacon for the vegetarians," Lauren suggested. "Because I think these are perfect as is, and I plan to eat a million more once they're on the menu."

"You got it! As long as you save some for the *other* vegetarians," Uncle Patrick said, and winked at Lauren before he turned to me. "How are you with drawing breakfast items?"

"Um, I'm not sure I ever tried it," I told him.

"I hoped you'd want to create the sign for the new flavor. Something that would grab people's attention when they enter. If this cupcake is popular, who knows, maybe I can expand to breakfast cupcakes too. Then people could eat cupcakes for breakfast, lunch, and dinner!"

"Cupcakes are an important part of a balanced diet," Lauren confirmed.

"I'll give it a try," I said.

Uncle Patrick handed me a pack of chalk and pointed toward the sign by the door. "There's your canvas; I can't wait to see the masterpiece you create!"

But what would make the drawing unique? Our art teacher, Ms. Suba, always said that when you're brainstorming, you put your first idea on hold and envision your second or third.

"The first one is always obvious," she'd say. "It's the common idea. The next few may be more unique, but it isn't until you dig deep that you find the perfect image to express your message. Those are the ones filled with magic. The real art from your heart."

"What's in my heart?" I asked myself as I stood in front of the chalkboard.

I thought of the obvious. A giant stack of pancakes. A bottle of syrup. Bacon. A kitchen table. Coffee. Morning. Sunrise.

"That's it!" I said, so loud that a woman in line turned and gave me a surprised look.

I drew the sun at the bottom. Then giant

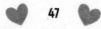

rays of light stretched above and beyond, filling almost the entire board.

I wrote *Eat Breakfast All Day* in bubble lettering big enough that it stood out against everything else.

I had stepped back to examine my work when the bell on the door jingled and a man's voice interrupted my thoughts.

"Whoa! Breakfast in the afternoon? Yes, please!" He walked straight to the counter and asked about the new cupcake flavor.

Success!

I wiped my palms on my jean jacket to get the chalk dust off and headed back to my friends. I gestured toward the man at the counter.

"Lauren, I'm not going to say I'm the reason why your uncle Patrick will make millions with this new flavor, but I'm also not going to deny it. That man walked in, saw my sign, and instantly ordered some pancake cupcakes."

"You're *totally* the reason," Lauren said, her mouth full of what had to be her hundredth cupcake.

"And it will be billions once he adds the bacon!" Ruby said.

"You could convince anyone to do anything with your art," Lauren said as she gestured at the man, who had now taken a big bite of his cupcake and looked very happy with his choice.

"Even to be nice?" Ruby asked, with a sneaky look in her eyes. She was up to something.

"What do you mean?" I asked.

"What if we chalked happy stuff onto the school playground? Everyone goes out there at least once a day for recess, and three times a day if they take the bus. We could fill it with positive messages to cancel out any future bad ones."

"Oh my gosh, oh my gosh! Yes!" Myka said. "I love it."

Myka was right—it was a great way to spread happy thoughts. We could cover every inch of that playground with positivity. I imagined what it would be like. Our classmates would head outside to play and notice the writing on the ground. Each person would begin to smile as they read the words. Soon the playground would be full of nothing but happiness, kindness, and love.

"It's perfect," I said. "Art can be our superpower in our fight against evil!"

"And good always triumphs over evil," Myka said.

Ruby picked up another cupcake and said, "Here's to the Invincible Girls!"

We grabbed cupcakes of our own and held them in the air.

"To the Invincible Girls!" Myka said.

As we smashed our cupcakes into each other and burst out laughing, I thought about how, through the magic of art, we might be able to change our school for the better.

And that was the true million-dollar idea.

6 ON YOUR MARK, GET SET, VAN GOGH SPREAD KINDNESS!

The four of us devised a plan to convince our parents to take us to the school the next afternoon. Except, it turned out we didn't need to do any convincing. They loved the idea. So much so that Ruby's grandma; Emelyn's mom; Myka's brothers Remy, Alex, and Jordan and her parents; and Lauren's mom and stepbrother, Carter, came with us to the playground.

"This is what I call a group effort!" Ruby said.

"We wouldn't have it any other way," Lauren's

mom said. "You girls come up with the best ideas ever."

Myka's dad held up a bag full of boxes of chalk. "I think it's safe to say there aren't any stores in town with chalk left on their shelves."

"I hope there isn't a teacher who's planning a big lesson tomorrow and needs some!" Ruby's grandpa joked.

"All right," Ruby said after Myka had done one of her loud whistles to get everyone's attention. "We are here on a mission. To spread positivity and kindness. You can write, draw, and decorate however you want. Just fill this space with happy thoughts!"

Our group cheered, grabbed chalk, and got to work. Remy had brought a portable speaker and cranked the volume, Lauren and Emelyn's moms passed out snacks, and we let our happy thoughts flow onto the asphalt. We laughed, sang, and talked as we worked, and I bet not one of us was thinking about mean messages and bullies. Instead we focused on the good.

"I don't think I've held a piece of chalk since I was in diapers," Remy said.

"*Since* you were in diapers? I thought you *still* wore them," Jordan said, and the two of them playfully wrestled with each other.

"Why are you drawing a hamburger?" Lauren asked Carter.

"I love hamburgers," he said. "Isn't the plan to draw things that make us happy? Trust me, other people feel the same. This hamburger will make anyone happy."

"In that case, I'll draw some dogs. There's nothing better than a dog, especially an older one," she said.

I turned back to the rainbow I was drawing and added a pot of gold at the end, because why not?

We wrote and drew until our chalk wore down to nubs and our fingers scraped against the asphalt.

We worked until the playground looked like a patchwork quilt of happiness.

It wasn't easy and took a few hours but was totally worth it.

Mom wiped her hands on her dress, leaving yellow streaks of chalk. "This is stunning!"

"It's our magnum opus!" Lauren declared.

We stared at her.

"Our what?" Myka asked.

"Magnum opus! It's from *Charlotte's Web*," she said. "It means our 'greatest work'!"

"That's for sure!" Myka agreed. "The Invincible Girls Club strikes again!"

"Is there anything the four of you can't do?" Lauren's mom joked.

"Nope!" Ruby said with a grin. "But we couldn't have done this without all of you. Thank you for your help."

"This makes me so happy," Myka said as she looked over the playground.

"It's a beautiful tribute to everyone who needs some positivity," Mom said.

I knew that the collage might not stop whoever

was writing the messages, but it covered the school with the good instead of the bad.

Because that was what art could do.

I slept well that night. For the first time in a few days, my head wasn't filled with the words of mean messages. Instead all I saw were our chalk drawings. I couldn't wait for everyone else to discover them too, and I fell asleep hopeful about what the morning would bring.

SINGING THE BLUES 7

The next morning brought disaster.

I swatted my alarm with my hand.

It took me a second to remember what we had done the day before. I threw off my covers and jumped out of bed, excited to see my classmates' reactions when they discovered our messages.

Except something wasn't right.

It was dark in my room.

Usually the sun was working its way into the sky and starting to stream through the cracks in my curtains when my alarm went off.

Had I set it wrong?

But that didn't make sense. Mom had set it a long time before, and I never touched it because I didn't want to mess it up.

I could also smell coffee, which was a sure sign it was morning. Mom never started the day without a pot of strong coffee.

That was when I heard it.

Thunder.

I pulled back my curtains and screamed. A big, loud, bloodcurdling, monster-was-chasing-me kind of scream.

Because what I saw outside was horrifying.

It was raining.

And not a gentle sprinkle.

No, it was a hard-pounding, giant-puddles kind of rain.

The kind that washes everything away.

 60

Including chalk drawings on the playground.

"Emelyn! Are you okay?" Mom asked as she burst into my room.

No, I wasn't okay.

Not at all.

I was crying so hard, it was impossible to get the words out and tell Mom why.

"The rain," I finally said. "It's ruined everything."

"Oh, honey," Mom said once she realized what I meant. She kneeled next to me. "I'm sorry. You put so much effort into the drawings."

And it was true. We had worked to turn things around at our school. To help others feel better instead of down in the dumps. And for what? It was being washed away before anyone even got to see it.

"Everything is gone," I said.

"Don't let that stop you," Mom told me.

"How can it not?"

"Remember how it felt yesterday when you

were done? Use that feeling to do something bigger. Something better."

"Better than that whole playground?"

"Better than the playground," Mom confirmed. "This stinks, but don't give up, honey. You can still do great things."

It was hard to believe Mom's words. We had chalked the playground for everyone else. It was supposed to make them feel better, and now it was gone. Poof! Washed away in an instant as if what we had to say wasn't important at all.

A PAINTBRUSH WITH THE LAW

8

"Strike one for the Invincible Girls," Myka said as the rain continued to fall all morning. No one could argue with that. Instead of watching the reactions of our classmates as they discovered what we had created, we were stuck inside. The gloomy day totally matched our feelings.

Miss Taylor rang the bell on her desk to get everyone's attention.

"We're stopping class early to welcome a visitor. Ms. Álvarez wants to talk to everybody."

Ms. Álvarez was one of my favorite people. She stood in the hallway at the start of each day and gave us high fives. She loved to play silly jokes on us, and she dressed like a different book character every Friday.

"Ohhhhhh, is Emelyn in trouble again?" Nelson said, and turned to some of his friends and laughed.

"Knock it off!" Myka said. "She was never in trouble. She was asked to take something to the office because she's responsible."

"All right, you two," Miss Taylor said. "This isn't about Emelyn, and I certainly hope it's not about anyone else in the class. Ms. Álvarez wants to talk about some messages that have been found throughout the school."

The class sat up straighter and quieted down. Miss Taylor was usually so nice that when she got serious, we listened.

"You're a good group of kids," she said. "I love all of you, and I'd be disappointed if I found out one of you was involved in this."

Before she could say anything more, there was a knock at the door.

"Ahhh, there she is."

Usually a visit from Ms. Álvarez was a treat, but today it was obvious that wasn't the case. She didn't have on her usual brightly colored outfit. Instead she had on a black suit, and there wasn't any trace of a smile on her face. She was what Mom would call "all business."

"Thank you for welcoming me, even if it's not for the best reason," she said. "I hate that I have to talk to the classes, but we've had some messages appear around the school that are hurtful and wrong. Some of you might have heard about them, some of you might have seen the latest ones, or some of you might know nothing about it. I want to apologize to anyone who has been affected by them. I don't have to remind you how seriously we take bullying. And these messages are most definitely bullying. A cowardly kind, and I won't stand for it. Whoever is doing this needs to stop."

I scanned the room. I couldn't imagine any of my classmates being that mean. But someone in the school was doing it, so I guessed it could have been one of us.

"A few things will change until there's a stop to this," Ms. Álvarez continued. "No one will be allowed in the hallway without a teacher. You'll move together as a group and have scheduled bathroom times. There will also be no hanging

 66

anything on the walls or the lockers. We hope these new rules will end things. I also suggest that if you're the one writing these messages, come forward. It would be better for you to talk to one of us now than to have us discover who you are."

Then she did that thing adults sometimes do to make you super uncomfortable. She studied each of us and didn't say a word. We squirmed in our seats. It was as if we were *all* in trouble.

Finally Ms. Álvarez said, "All right, I hope this is the only time I'll have to talk with you and we won't be seeing any more messages around the school."

Miss Taylor walked the principal to the door, and the entire class began to whisper at once.

Ruby turned to me, her eyes wide.

"Do you really think the person writing those messages could be in our class?"

"I hope not," I said as my eyes scanned the room, inspecting my classmates. I wrapped a piece of my hair around my finger and thought about the mean note about me. "I really hope not."

BACK TO THE
DRAWING BOARD

9

Being an Invincible Girl could mean doing big, giant, amazing things to change the world, but it could also mean doing small things that made a difference to a single group of people, which was why when I got to school the next day, I instantly fell in love with our club's newest idea.

"What are these?" I pointed to the little sheets of paper that covered my desk and my friends' desks. Each sheet had a message like the ones we had chalked on the playground. Messages full of kind and positive things. Words that would make people smile.

"Our wall of wonderful!" Lauren exclaimed. "Well, the start of it."

"It's our newest plan to stop the mean messages," Myka said, and gestured to her right, where Ruby sat. "Ruby came up with it."

"I don't mean to brag, but yep, I did!" Ruby said. "And it's brilliant."

"What is it?" I asked, eager to see what they wanted to do.

Ruby talked in an excited rush. "I love the drawings you made each of us, and I look at mine about a million times a day."

"Same here!" Myka said.

"They got me thinking that it would be amazing to make one for everyone in the school," Ruby told me.

"But impossible," Lauren said. "It would take foreeeeever."

"So Ruby thought of something else!" Myka said, and nodded at Ruby. "Tell Emelyn about it!"

Ruby rolled her eyes. "I'm trying to, but *someone* keeps interrupting. Anyways, I figured out a way to spread the same message without worrying about it getting washed away or taking forever. Our wall of wonderful!"

"What do you think? Isn't it genius?" Myka asked.

"Um, the messages are nice," I said. "But I still don't understand."

"So far I've created over fifty of them. I did it last night while my grandpa cooked, to keep him company," Ruby told me. "I thought we could create a ton more and hang them in the hallways."

I took a closer look at the messages. They were fun, goofy, and guaranteed to put anyone in a good mood. "So we cover the school with these?"

"Yep! All over! And since we're doing it inside, we don't have to worry about the rain," Myka said. "But that's not the best part! We want people to take them so they can put them in their notebooks and on their walls. Just like we did with the ones you made for us."

"We'll drown out the negative stuff," Lauren added.

"We'll wash away the bad with a tidal wave of good!" Ruby said, proud of her comparison.

"I love the idea," I told them.

"We hoped you would," Lauren replied. "And we've made you our official artist. You can draw pictures that will make people smile."

"I can totally do that," I agreed.

"Great!" Ruby said. "Now grab some paper and a marker and get drawing."

And that's exactly what I did. The four of us worked all day during any free time we could get and created so many little slips of paper that I was pretty sure we could cover every inch of the school, both inside and out!

PAINTING YOURSELF INTO A CORNER

10

"**W**e officially have three hundred and twenty-seven messages of positivity!" Myka declared at lunch the next day. We had brought to school the notes we'd created at home, and she had spent lunch counting them, in between bites of her sandwich.

"That's a ton of happy thoughts," Lauren said.

"I can't wait to see everyone's faces when they discover them," I told the group.

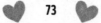

"I hate to be the one with the bad news, but we have a roadblock," Ruby said. "I thought of it last night."

"You always find a problem," Myka groaned.

"It's important to make sure our plans are executed perfectly," Ruby said. "That's how a good news reporter checks that her facts are accurate!"

"Ex-a-what?" Lauren asked.

"'Executed' means 'to carry out our plan,'" Ruby said. She loved to use big words, and thank goodness she didn't mind explaining them to us. "I know what is going to mess this up. Ms. Álvarez's rule. The fact that we can't be in the hallways. Remember, we have to move as a group."

Myka threw her hands up in frustration. "I didn't even think about that. When are we going to be able to hang them up?"

"Maybe we could do it after school?" Lauren suggested.

"I doubt we'd be allowed to stick around school at the end of the day," Ruby said. "Ms.

Álvarez made it clear we couldn't be anywhere on our own."

The four of us studied the stack of notes on the table. There had to be a way. Something we could do.

"I have an idea," Myka said. She stood and took her empty lunch tray to the drop-off window.

When she came back, she sat in her chair and grabbed at her foot.

"Did you see that?" she asked.

"See what?" Ruby said.

"I tripped. And I hurt my ankle. I can't put any weight on it *at all*."

"I didn't see you—" Lauren said, but Myka shushed her.

"Don't say anything," she said, and raised her hand.

Ms. Wamelink, one of the cafeteria monitors, came over, and Myka told her the same story, complete with lots of grimacing. "I don't think I can walk on it myself. Can my friends walk me to the nurse? I should probably ice it right away."

"Of course," Ms. Wamelink said. "Do you want me to help?"

"I think we've got it," Myka said, and gestured for us to gather around her. "I'll lean between Emelyn and Lauren. Ruby, can you carry my book bag?"

The three of us clustered around her.

"We've got this, Ms. Wamelink," Ruby said.

"Okay, if you're sure. Take it slow," she said.

"Oh, we will," Lauren promised.

We helped Myka out of the cafeteria, and I have to say, not only was she great at sports, but she was a phenomenal actress too. She hop-limped the entire time and scrunched her face in pain every now and then.

However, once we were out of the cafeteria and in the main hallway, Myka planted both feet on the ground.

"Whoa!" she exclaimed. "I seem to be healed!"

Lauren and I laughed.

"I can't say it was right to lie to Ms. Wamelink, but we got permission to be in the hallway alone," Ruby said.

"Now that we are, let's not waste any time. Who knows how long we have," Myka said.

"You're right," Ruby agreed. "Let's divide and conquer. Emelyn and I will take the main hallway, and Myka and Lauren, you can do the other two hallways. Everyone, remember the number one rule."

"Don't get caught?" Myka asked.

"Well, yeah, that's true. Okay, remember rules number one and two!" Ruby added. "Leave no inch of the school uncovered! Or, you know, cover as much as you can until you run out!"

It was fun to hang the positive messages, even though we could have gotten caught at any moment!

Ruby and I developed a routine. She held the tape and gave me pieces as I hung the papers. We moved through the halls fast and covered as much as we could.

I was a ninja, sneaky as I crept in the shadows.

No one could spot us.

We were too fast.

We were too sly.

We were—

"What do you two think you are doing?"

Busted.

I dropped the papers I had left, and Ruby let out a yelp of surprise.

It was Ms. Álvarez.

"I can't even believe what I'm seeing right now," she said.

Ruby quickly shook her head. "No, wait, you have it wrong. We were spreading positivity. We weren't doing anything wrong. I promise."

I held what was left of our papers out to Ms. Álvarez. "Take a look. We wanted to cancel out those awful messages with good ones. Our plan was to help."

She paged through the papers and took her time as she read each.

"I appreciate your good deed, but you need to remember the rules. No one is allowed to be in the hallway without a teacher. And nothing can be hung up. At all."

"We're sorry," Ruby said for the both of us. "We thought this would be okay."

"Rules are rules. If I bend them for you, other people will want them changed also." She gestured toward the walls. "I'll help you pull these down."

So as quickly as our messages had gone up, each of them came down, and like our chalk drawings, no one would ever see them.

I remembered the way it had felt when Chelsea and I had pulled the negative messages down, and this was nothing like that. There was no thrilling feeling or believing we were doing the right thing. Instead I was disappointed that yet another idea hadn't worked out for us. Maybe the Invincible Girls weren't so invincible after all.

As Ms. Álvarez walked us back toward the cafeteria, she rifled through the stack of notes we had pulled off the wall.

"These are good. Really good," she said. "A breath of fresh air after the other ones."

"That was our plan," Ruby said. "We wanted to do something nice to make everyone feel like they mattered."

"That's a lovely gesture," Ms. Álvarez said.

"It was Emelyn's idea," Ruby told her, and for

a second I thought she was about to get me in trouble. "She made this incredible art for each of us, with words to describe the things that make us special. We wanted our classmates to experience that too, so we made messages that they could take with them. Happy thoughts to carry around and remind them that they matter."

"What a lovely idea," Ms. Álvarez said. "I hate to throw these away after hearing that."

"They are awesome, huh?" Ruby asked.

"That's okay. You're right, we need to stick to your rules. We won't *hang* anything on the walls," I said, an idea forming.

Ruby tried to silence me with her eyes. I could tell she was confused, but I had this under control.

"What if instead we *painted* something on the walls?" I gestured to the wall that faced the school entrance. It was the first thing you saw when you walked inside. "Take a look at that blank space. All that gray is depressing."

Ms. Álvarez studied the area. "It could use a little color."

"And we're the girls to do it! What about a mural? Something bright and colorful and fun! We could sketch our idea first so you can approve it," I said.

"Yes!" Ruby said. "This is perfect! Emelyn would totally paint something worthy of a museum here!"

"There's a lot of empty space," Ms. Álvarez agreed. "And I like the idea of creating something positive that your classmates will see every day."

"You wouldn't regret it," Ruby said. "The four of us are a great team!"

"The four of you?" Ms. Álvarez asked.

Ruby gestured to the end of the hall, where Lauren and Myka were walking toward us. "It wasn't just Emelyn and I who hung the messages. Lauren and Myka were in the other hallways."

Ms. Álvarez threw up her hands. "Of course

you covered the entire school! How silly of me to think it was only one hallway."

"We're a package deal," Ruby said. "It's all or nothing."

"How did I go from the one making the decisions to trying to strike a deal with you?" Ms. Álvarez asked, but she was still smiling, so she wasn't mad.

"My mom says I can negotiate my way out of an alligator's mouth!" Ruby replied proudly. "So what do you say? Can we do it?"

"I don't see why not," Ms. Álvarez said. "I love that you're taking a stand and want to tell your classmates that you won't allow these negative things to happen."

"Not *tell*," I corrected her. "We want to *show* them."

And with that, my mind was already spinning with ideas of what we could create.

11

THINGS AREN'T ALWAYS BLACK AND WHITE

When you're excited about something, it's hard to keep quiet about it. The Invincible Girls and I talked about the mural project nonstop. Our desks were covered in sheets of paper with sketches, pencils, and crayons during any free time we had, and I found myself doodling ideas even when I was supposed to be working on assignments.

"What is that?" Rhiannon, a girl in our class, asked as she pointed to the drawing I'd made.

I couldn't help but fill her in.

"That sounds really neat," she said.

"It should be. I can't wait to see what it looks like when we're done!" I told her.

"People will walk by it all the time, and it will make them feel good," she said.

"Exactly!" I said. She totally got it.

"It would be cool to be a part of something like that," she said.

"Do you want to join us?" I asked. The Invincible Girls Club was all about including others, so I was sure the rest of the girls wouldn't mind another helper.

"I don't know if I should," Rhiannon said slowly, which confused me. A second before, she'd been totally into it.

"You should!" I said. "Join us on Sunday. It will be a blast."

She still hesitated, so I pushed a little more.

"I won't take no for an answer," I said. "The mural is supposed to bring people together, so it only makes sense for you to join us!"

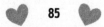

"Okay, I'd like to," she said shyly.

"Great! I can't wait," I said.

None of us could, which was why we continued to work on the drawing until it was absolutely perfect in our eyes.

On Friday, Ms. Blume walked us down to Ms. Álvarez's office so we could show her our design. It was pretty good, if I do say so myself, and while I'd been the one to sketch it, it had totally been a team effort.

We rushed to her office, giddy about what we had created.

"I hope she likes it," I said. Because while we loved what we had come up with, who knew if Ms. Álvarez would feel the same? And she was the one with the final say, so she could totally veto our idea.

"How could she not? Everything about it is stupendous," Lauren said, and I tried to believe in our art as much as she did.

"Hello, girls!" Ms. Álvarez said when we

entered her office. "I sure am hoping that sketch-book you have in your arms, Emelyn, contains the first mural ever to grace the halls of our elementary school."

"You'd better believe it," Ruby said.

"We've got something that is going to knock your socks off," Myka told her. "Wait until you see our design!"

"I cannot wait," Ms. Álvarez said. "Let's see what you've got!"

"Ta-da!" Myka exclaimed as I handed over the sketch of what we had done.

Ms. Álvarez studied it in silence. Finally, after what felt like an eternity, she looked at us. "Girls, I don't know what to say."

My stomach dropped.

She didn't like it.

"It's okay," I said. "It was just a draft. We can come up with something—"

"Whoa, whoa, whoa," Ms. Álvarez said. "I don't want anything else. I *love* everything about this!"

87

"You do?" I asked.

"Of course! It's better than I could have imagined!"

"Woo-hoo!" Myka shouted. "We were hoping you'd feel that way!"

"Let me know what you need so I can have it ready for you on Sunday," she said.

Ruby held up her notebook. "On it! We'll get you the list by the end of the day."

"Perfect," Ms. Álvarez said, and grinned. "I can't wait to see what it looks like up on the wall."

"It will be amazing," I promised, because with the Invincible Girls working together, there was no doubt we'd create something spectacular!

THE MURAL OF THE STORY

12

A week after we had chalked all over the playground, we were back to spending another Sunday at school. But this time we didn't have to worry about rain washing our creation away.

Ms. Álvarez planned to work in her office while we painted, and even said she'd buy us pizza for lunch. Pizza and a day of art? Yes, please!

"Have a great time and make some magic!" Mom said as I got out of the car.

89

"For sure!" I promised, and skipped off toward the school.

The other Invincible Girls and Rhiannon were already gathered at the wall where we would paint.

Myka grinned and waved. "Get over here. We're ready to go and need your expertise!"

Once I was with them, Ruby turned to us, all business. Or, at least I thought she planned to be all business. It turned out she had something else in mind.

"Okay, Emelyn," she said. "You're in charge. Let us know what we need to do to help you."

"I'm in charge?" I asked.

"You sure are," Ruby told me. "This is your specialty. Tell us how you make the magic happen, and we'll do it!"

I panicked. That was kind of a major thing. What if I got it wrong? What if I did something to ruin everything?

But what if you do an amazing job? What if

your art makes a difference? A second voice had fought its way into my head, and I liked the sound of that one a lot better.

"Okay, we've got this," I said. I pointed to Myka. "You can get the paint ready. Put a bunch in each tray. Ruby, set out the brushes and towels. Lauren and Rhiannon, if you're okay with it, you can fill up the cups with water. I'll get started on the sketch."

"Got it, coach!" Myka joked, and saluted me.

"Oh yeah, we are going to make some art!" Lauren agreed. "Watch out, Picasso. The Invincible Girls are about to leave our mark!"

"The Invincible Girls?" Rhiannon asked.

"It's the name we came up with for ourselves," Myka told her. "Because no one can stop us from doing great things. And now you're one of us too!"

Rhiannon stared at the ground with a worried look on her face.

"Is everything okay?" Lauren asked her.

"I'm not feeling too invincible right now," Rhiannon said. "Do you think we could talk about something?"

"Sure, what's up?" I asked.

"I have to tell you something, and if you want me to leave, I'll understand."

"Why would we want you to leave, silly? We'd never turn down an extra helping hand!" Myka told her.

"This might change your mind," Rhiannon said. She took a deep breath and let it out before talking again. "I was the one who hung up all those messages."

The four of us froze.

"The mean messages?" Myka asked, even though we all knew what Rhiannon meant.

Rhiannon nodded.

"You're kidding, right?" Ruby asked.

"It was stupid. I was stupid. I shouldn't have done it."

"You hurt a lot of people, including one of my best friends," Ruby said in a voice that wasn't mean but also wasn't the nicest.

I stared at the ground; it was too hard to look Rhiannon in the eye right then.

"Why did you do it?" Myka asked.

"I got tired of everyone calling me 'Bubble' and laughing about it," Rhiannon said. She pulled a tissue out of her pocket and blew her nose.

"Bubble" was the name some of the kids in the class called her after she got a giant piece of gum stuck in her hair. Miss Taylor couldn't get it out, and Rhiannon had to spend the day with a giant hunk of gum in her hair. She came back the next day with short hair and a new nickname.

"I thought you were okay with it," Myka said. "You laughed when people called you that."

"Would you like to be reminded of the worst day of your life?" Rhiannon asked. "People kept leaving pieces of gum in my desk or yelling 'Pop' when I walked past. I was so tired of it."

"I didn't know you were upset," Lauren said.

"It was awful. And when some of you laughed, everything was worse. So I don't know, I guess I wanted to make everyone else feel as bad as I felt."

"Your words really hurt me," I told her.

"I shouldn't have written those notes. They didn't help. In fact, it made me feel worse because I was hurting other people in the same way I'd been hurt."

"I'm sorry we laughed at your nickname. It won't happen again," Ruby said.

"And I'll never write a mean note again," Rhiannon said. "I promise."

"It was brave of you to say something to us," Lauren said, and I nodded. It would be hard to admit something like that.

"I'm glad you did," I said.

"I'm glad I did too," Rhiannon agreed. "If you

want me to leave, I understand. After all, I'm the reason you're all doing this."

"Maybe you started things with your notes," I said, "but now this idea to spread kindness through art has blown up. It's bigger than your notes at this point."

"A lot bigger," Myka said as she stretched her hands out against the wall where we planned to paint.

"And we still need help," I said, and gestured toward the rest of the Invincible Girls. "So as long as they're okay with it—"

"The more help the better," Lauren said.

Ruby nodded. "Yep, we'd like you to stay."

Rhiannon relaxed as if we had lifted a million-pound weight off her shoulders.

"I'd love to," she said, and we grinned.

"We all make mistakes, but we can also forgive," I said.

"On the count of three, let's do a giant group

apology," Myka said, and put her hand out, as if we were getting ready to play a sport.

I put my hand on top of hers, and the other girls did the same.

"One, two, three—SORRY!" we yelled, and dissolved into giggles.

A MASTERPIECE OF THE SOLUTION

13

The girls scattered to complete their assigned jobs, and I stood in front of the wall.

I picked up my pencil and sketched the first lines.

And guess what?

It felt good.

No, wait. It felt *really* good.

All of this did.

Because I was making a difference with my art!

And what could be better than that?

The five of us talked and joked as we painted. We were in an art trance.

We worked through the morning and only took a break to eat the pizza Ms. Álvarez ordered for us.

We painted all afternoon and continued as the light outside grew dim.

"We started as the sun came up and are finishing as it goes down!" Ruby said as she put the finishing touches on the lettering.

"A day full of art!" Myka cheered.

"Art with heart!" I said, which was the perfect way to describe what we had created.

And wow!

Had we created!

"This wall is officially a masterpiece," Rhiannon declared.

"Our magnum opus!" Lauren said.

The wall was now covered in bright, cheerful colors, a positive message, and a picture certain to make everyone smile.

"It's like the art is giving us a giant hug," Myka said.

Lauren ran to get Ms. Álvarez from her office.

"Are you ready for the big reveal?" I asked when I spotted the two of them heading toward us.

"I sure am! This is quite exciting," our principal said as she and Lauren walked down the hall. "I'm the first to view your work. I'm honored."

Myka made a trumpet noise with her mouth. "Ladies and . . . ladies . . . presenting the greatest work of art ever created! The cream of the crop! Numero uno! The prize-winning—"

"Okay, we get it," Ruby said, and we stepped aside so Ms. Álvarez could take it all in.

I had used inspiration from the day when we'd sat around the table at Sprinkle & Shine. I had taken the picture I'd chalked on the board that day and brought it back full circle. On the wall was a similar sunrise, but here it was huge. The rays of the sun stretched all the way to the ceiling. We had mixed glitter into some of the paint, and the edges sparkled. And on top of it, we had painted the words "SHINE BRIGHT."

"What do you think?" I asked hesitantly.

"It's stunning!" Ms. Álvarez said, and swiped at her eyes. I was pretty sure she had wiped away some tears. "You've surpassed my expectations! I can't wait for everyone to see this."

"Really?" I asked.

"Totally," Ms. Álvarez said. "No matter what is going on outside, the sun will always shine when you enter the school. This is exactly what the school needed."

And when I stepped back and took in the mural one more time, I realized she was right.

COLOR ME IMPRESSED

14

Mission accomplished!

Our painting was a success. In fact, the entire school could not stop talking about the new mural.

And the best part was that Ms. Álvarez had already hinted at wanting us to do more paintings around the school!

"Invincible Girls Club did it again," Ruby whispered to us. We were supposed to be going over our vocabulary definitions, but it was hard to focus on anything but what we had created.

"It's great to have people talking about good stuff," Lauren said, and I couldn't agree more.

There was a knock on the door and Ms. Blume walked in.

"Sorry to interrupt," she said. "But Emelyn, Lauren, Myka, Ruby, and Rhiannon are wanted in the office."

One person getting sent to the office was excitement enough, so you can imagine what happened when five people were sent there.

The class erupted.

"Again!" Nelson said, delighted. "And this time Bubble is going too!"

Rhiannon stood up and faced him. "Please stop calling me that. It's not my name."

"What? 'Bubble'?" he said with a goofy grin.

"My name is Rhiannon," she said.

Nelson held up his hands in surrender. "Sorry. I was just having some fun."

Rhiannon shook her head. "That wasn't fun. I

hate that nickname and would really like you to call me by my name."

I held my breath and waited for Nelson to say something nasty back, but instead he nodded.

"Fair enough," he said. "'Rhiannon' it is."

"Thank you," she said, and you could see the relief wash over her. I wanted to jump up and cheer. Part of being an Invincible Girl was standing up for yourself, and that was exactly what Rhiannon had done.

"Thank you for listening and respecting her wishes," Miss Taylor told Nelson. She nodded at us. "Go ahead, girls. I'll catch you up when you return."

When we hesitated, Ms. Blume smiled. "It's okay. I know for a fact that this is a good thing."

"We're going to hold you to that," Myka said.

"You've got my word," Ms. Blume said, and made a cross over her heart.

We all stepped into the hallway, and I told

myself it was okay. I trusted Ms. Blume.

We turned the corner to the office, and there on the wall around our painting were brightly colored squares.

Notes exactly like the ones that had been stuck all over the school by Rhiannon.

My heart dropped.

I met Rhiannon's eyes, but she shook her head quickly.

"I don't know what's going on," she said.

If those notes were bad, I didn't want to see this.

I *couldn't* see it.

"Earth to Emelyn," Myka said, and tickled me in the side. "Get over here. You're missing this."

"I'll pass," I told her.

Myka tickled me harder.

"Stop that!" I said, and wiggled away from her fingers.

"You need to look at this, silly," she said. "It's a good thing."

Reluctantly I walked over to the wall.

"Wait, these are our messages," I said.

"Yep, the ones that Ms. Álvarez took from us, and a whole bunch of new ones."

They surrounded the mural, each stuck to the wall with a brightly colored piece of tape.

If the painting we had created was a hug, then this was a giant bear hug. The kind where the person picks you up and squeezes so hard that you think you might pop. The kind of hug that warms your body from the inside out and lets you know you're not alone. Lets you know that you're loved and supported.

Ms. Blume beckoned to us to follow her into the office, but the five of us hesitated at the door and exchanged looks. Then Myka grabbed my hand and pulled me in. Lauren and Ruby followed.

I reached out and clasped Rhiannon's hand, pulling her into our group.

As we entered, a strange thing happened.

People began to clap.

It was slow at first. But soon the entire office was on their feet and clapping for us.

Ms. Álvarez was the loudest. She came over to us and gestured for everyone to be quiet.

"Girls, thank you for the amazing art you created. This school is a better place because of what you designed."

I was proud that I had used my art for good, because while words can make a person feel awful about themselves, art can give us hope and remind us of how amazing we can be.

And that's exactly what the Invincible Girls had set out to do.

"You held on to our pieces of paper," Ruby said.

"I couldn't throw them away. I loved the idea you talked about of carrying around positive messages with you. The entire staff added more to the wall, and I'm hoping we continue the trend and kids can create messages of their own and take one off the wall whenever they feel like they need it."

"That's the perfect idea!" I said. "Now everyone can carry around a little bit of happy, and what could be better than that?"

"Before we can completely celebrate, though, there's one small problem," Ms. Álvarez told us. "We're missing a very important element."

"We are?" I asked, worried I'd messed up somehow. "What is it?"

"Your names!" she said, and held up a permanent marker. "We need to know who created this."

I relaxed. That was an easy fix.

"You first," Myka said, and gave me a nudge toward the mural.

I took the marker and signed my name. Then, my friends and Rhiannon did the same, their names surrounding mine.

It felt like a hug.

And that was perfect.

Ms. Álvarez held up a fancy camera. "Now let's take a few pictures of all of you by your mural."

We slung our arms around each other. As we did, I noticed a piece of paper with the word "UNSTOPPABLE" written on it.

I pulled it off and put it in my pocket.

"Unstoppable," I said out loud when Ms. Álvarez asked us to smile.

Yep, that's exactly what the Invincible Girls were.

And as the camera flashed, I thought, *Just wait until you see what we do next.*

Hello, Amazing Reader!

If you've hung with the Invincible Girls Club before, welcome back! If this is your first time meeting Lauren, Myka, Ruby, and Emelyn, I'm glad to see you here!

The four of them are so passionate about making a difference, and I hope they inspire you to want to create change in your school, your community, and the world!

Because remember, you're never too young to make an impact.

We *all* have the potential to change the world.

We *all* have the ability to do great things, big and small.

We can *all* be invincible.

So, if you haven't joined the club yet, let me extend an official invitation to come together and show the world what the Invincible Girls Club can do! We are only as strong as the girl next to us, so come, let's stand together and make some change!

Love,

Rachele Alpine

aka . . . a lifetime member of the Invincible Girls Club!

MEET
INVINCIBLE GIRL
Amy Burkman

Amy is an American artist known for the murals she creates (similar to the one the Invincible Girls made!) and her speed paintings. She makes images on giant canvases in front of audiences in less than ten minutes. She travels and performs in many different countries as a way to raise money and support important causes. She even started a nonprofit called Good Art Project and has donated nearly one million dollars. Amy is an Invincible Girl because she's using her artistic talents to raise money for global conservation and to inspire change in the world.

INVINCIBLE GIRL

Frida Kahlo

Frida was a Mexican artist whose country and culture heavily influenced her art. She loved to paint in bright colors, and many of her works were self-portraits. Frida was sick for much of her life and was in a bad accident that affected her body in many ways. She used painting as a way to express how she was feeling both physically and emotionally. Frida was an Invincible Girl because at the time when she was painting, not many women were artists. She didn't let that stop her, though. She wanted to share her incredible art and its messages with the world.

INVINCIBLE GIRL

Amy Sherald

Amy is an American painter whose focus is portraits. She uses her art as a way to tell the stories of contemporary Black Americans. She was the first woman and the first African American to win the National Portrait Gallery's prestigious Outwin Boochever Portrait Competition. Michelle Obama loved the work Amy did, so she selected Amy to paint her official portrait. Amy is an Invincible Girl because of the power of her paintings and the stories she tells through her portraits.

MEET
INVINCIBLE GIRL

Yayoi Kusama

Yayoi Kusama is a Japanese artist who is best known for her installations, many of them rooms that you can enter and experience. She loves to use bright colors and shapes, especially polka dots and pumpkins! Her pieces often have an anti-war stance and celebrate females and equal rights.

119

Her Infinity Mirror Room exhibits welcome viewers into a series of dark boxes where she uses mirrors and lights to make it seem as if life goes on forever. Yayoi is an Invincible Girl because she is an innovator in the art world, both as a woman and through the messages she creates with her work.

MEET
INVINCIBLE GIRL
Phoebe Wahl

Phoebe is an award-winning American author and illustrator of children's books. Her images focus on the relationship between people and nature. She most often uses watercolors and collage to create gorgeous images of animals, flowers, and plants. Phoebe also uses her art to be an advocate

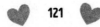

for equality and body positivity. She believes that everyone is beautiful and worthy of love and respect. Phoebe is an Invincible Girl because she uses her artistic talents to celebrate the people and world around her and teaches young readers to do the same.

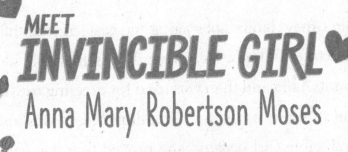

MEET
INVINCIBLE GIRL
Anna Mary Robertson Moses

This Invincible Girl was known by the nickname "Grandma Moses." She didn't begin to paint until she was seventy-eight years old, but once she started, she quickly gained popularity. The style of painting that she did was called folk art, and it featured old-fashioned towns or what she called "old-timey" landscapes along the eastern coast of the United States. Her artwork was first sold at county fairs and then was used for greeting cards and hung in museums. Grandma Moses was an Invincible Girl because she proved that you can be awesome at any age!

MEET
INVINCIBLE GIRL
Faith Ringgold

Faith Ringgold is an artist who was raised in Harlem, New York, in a house that was heavily influenced by the Harlem renaissance. She was encouraged to be creative by her family and was surrounded by all types of art growing up. She has created quilts as a way not only to express herself but also to share the stories of African American history. In addition to making quilts, Faith has worked alongside her daughter Michele to fight against racism and for equal rights for women. Faith is an Invincible Girl because she found a way to make her voice heard through art.

MEET
INVINCIBLE GIRL
Addy Rivera Sonda

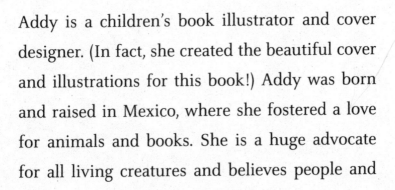

Addy is a children's book illustrator and cover designer. (In fact, she created the beautiful cover and illustrations for this book!) Addy was born and raised in Mexico, where she fostered a love for animals and books. She is a huge advocate for all living creatures and believes people and animals should coexist peacefully. She uses her illustrations to fight for animal rights and to inspire others to love and care for animals as much as she does. Addy is an Invincible Girl because she uses her talent to educate others about the importance of taking care of our earth and sharing it with all the animals and critters who inhabit our air, water, and land.

MEET
INVINCIBLE GIRL
Sarah C. Rutherford

Sarah is a New York artist who uses giant murals to spotlight women who are helping other women. She created the public art project Her Voice Carries, which includes murals painted on the sides of buildings to celebrate females who empower and support others. Her project started in her hometown of Rochester, New York, but this is a movement that she hopes to spread throughout the United States. Sarah is an Invincible Girl because of the attention and celebration her murals provide for women of all races and backgrounds who are making a difference in our world.

MEET
INVINCIBLE GIRL
Akiane Kramarik

Akiane is an American painter who is said to be the youngest prodigy in realistic art. She started to sketch at age four and painted one of her most famous pictures, *Prince of Peace*, when she was eight. Since then she has created hundreds of paintings, many of which have sold for large sums of money. She has donated to over two hundred charities and says, "I want people to find hope in my work." Akiane is an Invincible Girl because she uses her talents to spread happiness and love in the world.

Ways That You Can Be an Invincible Girl and Help Change the World with Art!

- ❤ Create a group mural at your school, local playground, or community building.
- ❤ Make your own word picture for your friends like Emelyn did. See how many good things you can write about them!
- ❤ Hand-make cards for people in the hospital, in nursing homes, or serving in the military overseas.
- ❤ Get permission from local businesses to paint the windows with uplifting messages and images.
- ❤ Chalk positive messages on your driveway. (Or go to a friend's house and surprise them with messages and drawings on their driveway!)
- ❤ Write a letter to a friend you haven't talked to in a long time. Decorate the letter and envelope with drawings.

- ♥ Leave new coloring books and boxes of crayons around for kids to find. Leave a note encouraging the new artist to take them and drop them off in locations such as tables at the library, a restaurant, park bench, or doctor's office waiting room. Or better yet . . . create your own coloring book by drawing pictures in black marker.

- ♥ Gift a "Jar of Happy!" Fill a mason jar with pieces of paper that have drawings, quotes, and kind words. Give it to someone special. (They can pull out a piece of paper each time they need it!)

- ♥ Paint a flowerpot and then plant a flower in it. Give it to a friend or neighbor to spread some cheer.

- ♥ Create postcards to send. (You can either color them or leave them uncolored for your recipient to color in!)

- ♥ Donate books about artists to your school library.

- Give art supplies as a birthday gift to inspire creativity!
- Help create an art show (either in-person or digital) with pieces of art that promote kindness and love.
- Make color-by-number pictures or drawings that can be traced, for kids with special needs.
- Instead of buying holiday, birthday, or thank-you cards . . . design your own!
- Learn about an Invincible Girl artist and then mimic her style of art.
- Slip postcards or index cards with positive pictures and messages into your classmates' lockers. Encourage them to do the same!
- Create a community "quilt" that's made by piecing together drawings made by a group of people.
- Kindness rocks—paint rocks with happy messages and images, then hide them all over for people to find.

- Design bookmarks with positive messages and pictures. Hide them in books at your local library, school library, or Little Free Library.

- Collect old crayons, pull the wrappers off, and melt them. (Have an adult help!) Pour them into molds so you can use them again!

- Traveling picture—start with an image on a piece of paper and pass it on to other people. Each person must add something to the picture.

- Have an art scavenger hunt in your community. Everyone creates art centered around a theme and hangs their masterpieces in their windows. You then get to go on family walks and try to find them!

- Make art and sell it to your family and friends. Donate the money you make to your favorite charity.

- Lunch bag art—decorate lunch bags with fun and supportive messages.

- Make signs with positive messages and hang them over the mirrors in the girls' bathroom or post them on the inside of the stalls. (Make sure to get permission first!)
- Gather bags of art supplies (crayons, markers, construction paper, coloring books . . .) for kids in the hospital.

Turn the page for a sneak peek at the next book!

THE INVINCIBLE GIRLS • CLUB

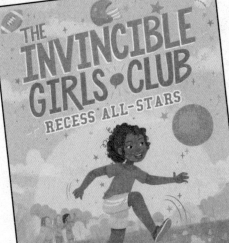

THE INVINCIBLE GIRLS • CLUB

RECESS ALL-STARS

by RACHELE ALPINE

illustrated by ADDY RIVERA SONDA

STRIKING OUT

Today was the day.

I could feel it in my bones.

Well, I could feel it in my legs, which were aching from the nonstop pumping I'd been doing.

Today was the day I would go all the way over the top bar of the swing set on our playground.

Many at Erie Elementary had tried, but none had succeeded.

I was about to change that.

I, Myka Bader, was ready to go for the glory.

This was what I had been preparing for, every day at recess.

I had come to school prepared. I'd chosen my soccer shorts, which were loose and billowy, and a T-shirt that was way too big that belonged to one of my older brothers. I hoped both would give me an extra push in the wind like the sail on a boat. I had also snuck my soccer cleats into my bookbag and put them on just before we'd gone outside. I'd wanted to make sure I got maximum traction when I pushed off.

My feet kicked up little puffs of dirt as I gained momentum.

I gripped the chains so tight, it was as if someone had superglued my hands to them.

Higher and higher I went. I swear, my feet almost skimmed the bottom of the white cotton-candy clouds in the sky.

My best friends—in the Invincible Girls Club—and I had planned it out.

Emelyn, who loved science, had calculated how fast and high I'd have to go to make it over the bar. Ruby had her camera ready to document it and planned to write an article about it for our elementary school newspaper, and Lauren had promised a victory party at her uncle's cupcake shop, Sprinkle & Shine.

I wasn't afraid.

Nope. Myka Bader wasn't scared of anything.

Well, okay, maybe I was a little teeny bit.

Who wouldn't be? The swing set was massively tall, and I was about to catapult myself over it on a tiny piece of rubber and chains.

But what was life without a little adventure?

"Pump! Pump! Pump!" Lauren and Emelyn shouted from below.

"Higher! Higher! Higher!" Ruby added in between their chants.

Other girls stood around clapping and bouncing from foot to foot as they waited to witness the event of a lifetime.

I had an entire cheering squad, and I refused to disappoint them.

One more pump, and I'd fly over the bar like a bird and come back down, the twisted chains around the top a memorial to my great feat.

Kids would talk about me for centuries.

I'd become a local legend.

Teachers would include me in their history lessons.

The school would place a plaque next to the swing set to honor my accomplishment.

"Ready or not, here I go!" I yelled.

The Invincible Girls Club cheered louder.

All I had to do was go a little bit higher. Pump a little bit harder . . .

TWEEEEEEEEEEEEEEEEEEEEEEEEEEEEEEET!

"Myka Bader, you slow down this instant!" a voice demanded. "You know the rules. You can't swing that high!"

I groaned.

Ms. Kratus.

The recess monitor.

Also known as . . . the destroyer of fun.

I was almost certain that if there was a good time to be had, Ms. Kratus could sniff it out and stop it in its tracks. Every. Single. Time. She was never without her whistle, which she used for ultimate recess torture.

We couldn't throw snowballs in the winter, dodgeball had been banned, and once she had even tried to stop us from pretending that the ground was lava, as if we were running through actual lava. There was no doubt in my mind that if she could make it happen, she'd demand we take naps during recess.

"How many times do I have to tell you not to swing that high?" she demanded, and I was smart enough to know that was a question I wasn't supposed to answer.

I slowed down and jumped off the swing in midair.

TWEEEEEEEEEEEEEEEEEEEEEEEEEEEEEEEET!

"No jumping off the swings!" she added as my dreams of becoming a playground legend were officially destroyed.

I stomped over to my friends. "It's so unfair! She never lets us have any fun."

"What a bummer," Emelyn said.

"You were totally about to go over," Lauren added.

"Don't worry," Ruby whispered. "You can try again in a few days when she's not looking."

"I'll be watching you, Myka!" Ms. Kratus said, as if she could hear our conversation.

"Or maybe not," Ruby said, and frowned.

I gestured toward the field, where a big group of boys was playing kickball. "I should join them. Then I can have some fun."

"You should!" Lauren agreed. "You're always so good when we play in gym."

"You're right," I said, and while it might have sounded as if I were bragging a little, it was true.

I watched them throw the ball and run around the bases.

Kickball.

Maybe my plan to go over the top of the swings was over, but I could be known for something else.

Myka Bader, the kickball all-star.

The one everyone fought to have on their team.

The one that everyone took giant steps back in the field for because my kicks were so powerful!

The one who *always* scored.

I liked the sound of that.

As I made my way toward the boys, I watched Nelson at home plate. His foot connected right in the sweet part of the ball, and it sailed up into the air toward me.

"I've got it!" I yelled, and ran forward with my hands outstretched. The ball landed in my arms with a satisfying *thunk*, and I held it over my head like a prizefighter showing off her trophy.

Except I appeared to be the only one excited about the catch.

"Why did you do that?" Nelson demanded.

"Yeah! You cost us a potential win. Syed could have scored, and we would've been ahead," Brady complained.

I held the ball, not sure what to do.

Nelson came over and took it.

"I didn't mean to mess up your game," I told him. "I saw the ball coming and, well, I wanted to play."

"Play?" he asked.

"I'm on the soccer team," I said. "I have a strong kick. Tell me where you want me to aim, and I should be able to get the ball right there!"

I pretended to kick a ball to show him that I had what it took.

"This is *our* game and our field," Brady said. "The girls have the playground."

Wait.

He didn't want me to play because I was a *girl*?

"You're joking, right?" I asked. "Since when is the field only for boys?"

"It's always been our place," Nelson said.

"Um, why?" I asked.

"Because that's the way it is." Nelson turned his back to me and threw the ball to those waiting in the infield. "Okay, Keagan, you're up!"

I made a face at Brady's back and marched back to my friends.

Ridiculous!

Maybe that was the way it had always been, but that most certainly wasn't the way it would stay.

Nope.

Not at all.

There was no reason why we girls couldn't play too. It was time to change things.

And I knew who could help.

I needed to call a meeting of the Invincible Girls Club.